Blyton's TOYLAND™

DON'T BLAME NODDY!

This edition first published in Great Britain by HarperCollins Publishers Ltd in 1999

1 3 5 7 9 10 8 6 4 2

ISBN: 0 00 136123 6

Cover design and illustrations by County Studio

Printed and bound in Hong Kong

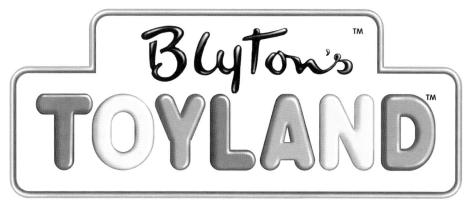

DON'T BLAME NODDY!

Collins

An Imprint of HarperCollins*Publishers*

It was very early in the morning and most of
Toy Town was still fast asleep. But not Big-Ears.
He was wide awake. And he was in such a state!

It had been a very hot night and Big-Ears had left all his windows open. While he was sleeping, someone had crawled in and stolen his purse full of sixpences!

"I *thought* I heard some sort of noise!" he wailed to himself. "Oh, why didn't I get up instead of just rolling over and going back to sleep?"

Luckily, Mr Plod was cycling past at that moment. He was doing his early morning patrol to make sure everything in the wood was just as it should be.

"Now, what's all this then, Big-Ears?" Mr Plod asked as he jumped off his bicycle.

Big-Ears told Mr Plod all about the robbery in the middle of the night. He was still very upset.

Big-Ears scratched his head.

"But they can't be," he said. "Not dear old Noddy's. They simply can't be."

"Oh, they're Noddy's all right," Mr Plod said. "No one else's shoes make footprints like these. I'm going straight to his house to arrest the young scamp!"

Big-Ears cycled with Mr Plod to Noddy's house. He still found it hard to believe that it was Noddy who had stolen his purse. Noddy was his best friend!

Luckily, Mr Plod was cycling past at that moment. He was doing his early morning patrol to make sure everything in the wood was just as it should be.

"Now, what's all this then, Big-Ears?" Mr Plod asked as he jumped off his bicycle.

Big-Ears told Mr Plod all about the robbery in the middle of the night. He was still very upset.

"Just leave it to me, Big-Ears," Mr Plod told him, starting to look for clues. "We'll soon have your purse back. Ah! Muddy footprints!" he cried suddenly. "All we have to do now is work out who they belong to!"

They both examined the footprints closely.

"Do you know?" Big-Ears said with surprise,
"I do believe those footprints are -"

"NODDY'S!" cried Mr Plod. "I was
just about to say so myself!"

Big-Ears scratched his head.

"But they can't be," he said. "Not dear old Noddy's. They simply can't be."

"Oh, they're Noddy's all right," Mr Plod said. "No one else's shoes make footprints like these. I'm going straight to his house to arrest the young scamp!"

Big-Ears cycled with Mr Plod to Noddy's house. He still found it hard to believe that it was Noddy who had stolen his purse. Noddy was his best friend!

When they reached Noddy's house, Noddy was only just getting out of bed.

"Hello, Big-Ears! Hello, Mr Plod!" Noddy said, with surprise as he opened the door. He stretched his arms. "You're both up early, aren't you?" he asked with a big yawn.

"Not as early as you were, young man!" Mr Plod exclaimed as he marched straight into Noddy's house and picked up his shoes. "Ah, just as I thought! Your shoes are covered with fresh mud. So it *was* you who stole Big-Ears' purse!"

"I most certainly did not -" Noddy began. But then he saw Mr Plod reaching for his handcuffs. Poor Noddy became scared. Even though he was still in his pyjamas and bare feet, he ran out of the door.

"Thief! Thief! Someone stop that thief!" Mr Plod shouted as he chased after him.

"I'm not a thief, I didn't steal Big-Ears' purse," Noddy cried, becoming more and more unhappy. He was so upset that he didn't see Milko walking along the road delivering the morning's milk.

CRASH!

Broken milk bottles rolled everywhere. Milko was furious, and shook his fist. But Noddy just kept running. He really didn't want to be arrested!

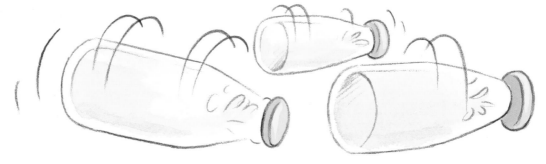

Now Big-Ears joined the chase after Noddy.
He had stayed behind in Noddy's house so that
he could have a closer look
at Noddy's shoes. But now he
ran down the road too, panting
and waving his arms.

"Stop, Noddy! Stop!"
he cried.

However, Noddy would
not stop. He ran and ran.

"Oh, be careful!" Sally Skittle cried as Noddy ran straight into all the little skittles on their way to school. "Oh dear! Oh dear! My poor children!"

The skittles were sent flying all over the place. They really didn't mind, though. In fact, there was nothing they liked better. But it caused such a *commotion!*

"Stop Noddy!" cried Mr Plod.

"Stop Noddy!" cried Milko.

"Stop, Noddy!" cried Big-Ears, trailing behind the others.

The next person Noddy ran into was Mr Wobbly Man. And as Noddy turned a corner he realised he was heading straight for Tessie Bear as well. Her hat had blown off and she was bending down to pick it up.

"Out of the way, Tessie! Out of the way!" Noddy cried.

Tessie didn't hear him, though. It looked as if Noddy would have to charge right into her. Mr Plod and the others had turned the corner by now and they were right behind him...

Suddenly, Noddy stopped. He couldn't knock down dear Tessie!

"I give up, Mr Plod," he sobbed, sadly holding out his arms.

Mr Plod was about to put his handcuffs on Noddy when Big-Ears finally caught up.

"Just wait a minute, Mr Plod!" he cried. Big-Ears held up a long green sock. "I found **THIS** in one of Noddy's shoes," he said.

"But it's not my sock," said Noddy, puzzled.

"I know it isn't," replied Big-Ears. "It belongs to Gobbo the goblin. Tell me, Noddy, did you do what I did and leave some of your windows open last night?"

Noddy had a think for a moment, then nodded his head.

"Just as I thought!" Big-Ears exclaimed. "Gobbo must have secretly borrowed your shoes so that he would leave *your* footprints when he robbed my house and not his own. But he made the big mistake of leaving a sock in one of them!"

Mr Plod started to write down everything that Big-Ears was saying. "I think I'd better pay that wicked goblin a visit!" he announced finally in a stern voice.

Noddy was very relieved. "You mean I won't be getting those handcuffs after all?"

"All you'll be getting, Noddy," laughed Big-Ears, "is a big reward! Won't he, Mr Plod? After all," he chuckled, "it wasn't really me who provided the vital clue but you. I might have found Gobbo's sock, but it was in your shoe!"

THE NODDY CLASSIC LIBRARY
by Enid Blyton ™

Available in hardback
Published by HarperCollins